This Young Family Center
material provided by
Hampton's
Healthy Families Partnership.

THE Cabbage Soup SOLUTION

ERIKA OLLER

DUTTON CHILDREN'S BOOKS

NEW YORK

To my dear daughter, Monica,
who has taught me how to eat my vegetables

CIP Data is available.

Published in the United States by Dutton Children's Books,
a division of Penguin Young Readers Group
345 Hudson Street, New York, New York 10014
www.penguin.com

Designed by Tim Hall
Manufactured in China
ISBN 0-525-47005-0
First Edition
1 3 5 7 9 10 8 6 4 2

Elsie lived a simple life on a small farm, with her two cats, Fluff and Gordo, for company. She grew potatoes, tomatoes, peas, and pumpkins. But growing cabbages was what Elsie did best.

Early each morning, when her little house was still chilly and dark, Elsie got up, put on her robe, and warmed herself with a steaming cup of tea. She gave Fluff and Gordo their breakfast of warm milk.

As the sky grew lighter, she would bundle up, gather her baskets, and go out to the field to collect the largest cabbages.

Fluff and Gordo always
came along to help.

Then she would load her truck and drive to town to sell her cabbages to the greengrocer. She had done this for years.

One morning, as usual, Elsie went out to her field.
But there was nothing usual about what she saw.

Half of her cabbages were gone!
Only ragged stumps were
left in their place.

For a moment,
she lost control.

But soon she pulled herself together.
She would not cry over shredded cabbages.

"Who could have done this?" she asked herself.
She had to try and find out.

That night, the cats went to sleep on Elsie's bed, as usual.
But Elsie decided to stay out in the field and watch for trouble.

Before long, though, she fell asleep.

In the morning, Elsie awoke stiff, cold, and cranky
to a field of messy new stumps.

She felt defeated. She also felt a cold coming on, so she dragged herself into the house for a hot cup of tea and a long nap.

Elsie slept all day.

But the cats took action.

Night came, and still Elsie slept. Fluff and Gordo didn't join her. They had some work to do.

The next morning, Elsie woke up feeling much better. She had only a small tickle in her throat. "I'll just have to plant more cabbages," she told her cats, who were unusually sleepy.

First, though, she would make a big batch of cabbage soup to soothe her throat.

When she stepped outside to pick some other vegetables, Elsie found a surprise by her door.

All of her soup ingredients were waiting for her in a neat little pile. "Well, wasn't that thoughtful," she said. "Someone decided to save me some trouble."

She put all of the vegetables in a huge pot, together with her last cabbage. "Might as well make extra for later," she said to Fluff and Gordo.

The smell of the soup filled the little house
as it simmered all day.

When Elsie sat down to eat supper, she saw that she wasn't alone.

"Now would you look at that," she said to Fluff and Gordo. "We have visitors."

She invited them in for some soup.
The cats chose to have fish for dinner instead.

After supper, with bellies full, everyone fell fast asleep.

The next day, Elsie told Fluff and Gordo,
"Time to plant new cabbages."

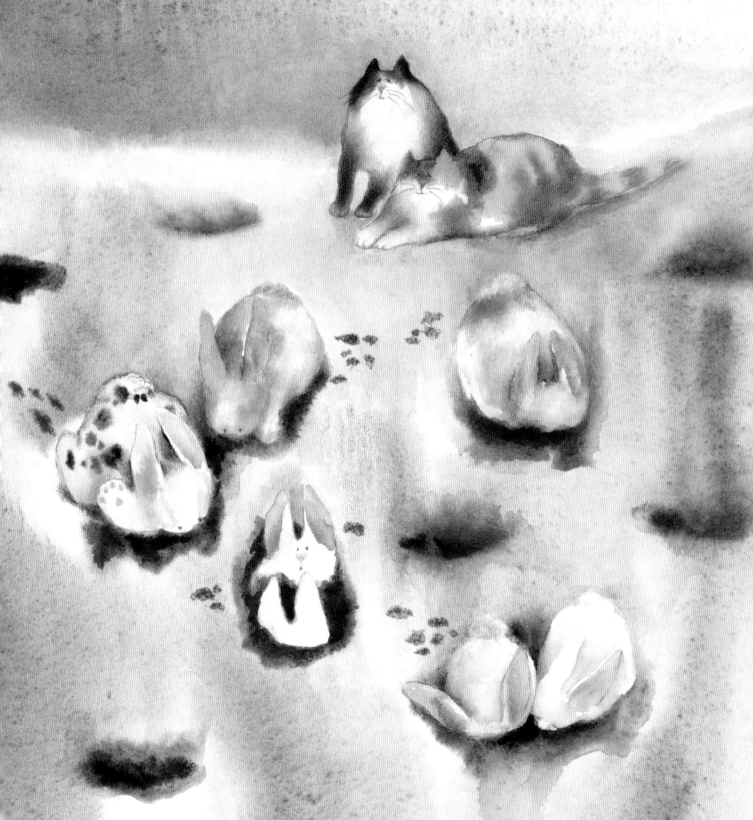

The cats made sure the rabbits helped. They dug holes for the plants, and even added a little fertilizer here and there.

Elsie's new cabbages grew and grew. They were better than ever, and there were plenty of them.

Plenty for Elsie...

plenty for the greengrocer...

and more than plenty for her new friends.

People heard about Elsie's beautiful cabbages and stopped by to take a look. Elsie made even more new friends—and more of her delicious cabbage soup.

Her life was no longer so simple, and she liked it that way. Best of all, the little house was always warm at night.